TO JOHN 9 THAN

F

Cc

Jack Connolly

Spectrum Versus The League of Conveniently-out-of-Copright-Villains

Illustrations by: Jack Connolly

Graphic Design & Cover Design by: Sinéad Poznanski

Available to buy: Amazon

ISBN-10: 1547124946

ISBN-13: 978-1547124947

SPECTRUM

VERSUS

THE LEAGUE OF CONVENIENTLY OUT-OF-COPYRIGHT VILLAINS

DEBUT SEMI-GRAPHIC NOVEL BY

JACK CONNOLLY

FOREWORD

Today is a very special day. I am publishing my first ever book. I like writing down my thoughts and ideas from my dreams. In my dreams terrible things happen. Sometimes I dream all my teeth are falling out, or that my gums and cheek are missing. In some dreams I am chased or I am falling. Once I had a dream that there were rats living in a pool under my bed. Other dreams are pleasant like visiting a different version of places I know or seeing comic book heroes. I also day-dream and invent characters and adventures. I like comic books so I have written this book as a semi-illustrated novel.

I would like to give special thanks to my Dad, my sister Michaela, Auntie Néady, and all my past teachers including Ian Scott, Fiona O'Donovan and Lynda Smyth.

About the Author

Jack Connolly is a twenty one year old self declared eccentric, who lives in Dublin, Ireland with his parents and three siblings. Jack was born with autism and has OCD. He is currently studying in the Ronanstown Community Training & Education Centre (Stuarts Care Ltd). The staff there have all been so supportive of Jack over the past three years in general and with this project in particular.

Jack has been very lucky throughout his life to have had some wonderful teachers. Under the nurturing guidance of Ian Scott in his outreach class in Lucan Educate Together, Jack was encouraged to pursue his writing skills and interest in Peter Pan when he adapted the story for a school play. In an environment where the child always comes first, the teachers and staff at the school always encouraged Jack to enhance his talents and follow his dreams. His love of Star Wars and Diary of a Wimpy Kid encouraged his reading, writing and drawing skills from an early age.

Jack is a huge fan of Batman and loves reading the comic books and watching all the movies. He is like a walking version of a Batman-Wikipedia.

Jack's writing is in many ways biographical but his cheeky sense of humour and amazing memory for facts and events allows him to draw on occurrences that happen around him. He is currently developing the plot for his next book.

For Grandad Big D

Boris Rhys Eli Ronald Quatermaine

from Pontypool in Wales

CHAPTER ONE

MEET BORIS

The first character in this book is from Pontypool in Wales and he is named Boris Rhys Eli Ronald Quatermaine. Boris's father was Welsh and his mother was Russian. They met at the Millennium Dome in London on New Years Eve 1999. Mr Robert Ioan (Welsh for John) Quatermaine used to work as a waiter, but when Boris was born he became his fulltime carer. Mrs Ivana Quatermaine worked as an assistant manager in laser tag. She said Boris got his autism from his Dad, who liked to collect action figures and used batteries, but his Dad said autism isn't contagious and if it was, they would all have it by now.

Boris lived in a one-bedroom flat with his mother and father. When he was five his mother had a baby boy called William. Everyone in the block of flats came for a party to celebrate. Ivana didn't care who was invited. The flat thumped with 1990's German trance "duff! duff!" music.

The TV got broken when a bottle was thrown at it by a fat bearded guy dancing like an orangutan. The floor looked like a war zone with broken glass.

Meanwhile, social worker Alun Jones was walking along the street and looked up to see which flat the loud music was coming from. His eyes popped out of this head when he saw a fat bearded guy dangling a crying baby upside-down out of the window. He ran as fast as he could to catch the baby with his arms out-stretched. “What you are doing you stupid prat!” Luckily the baby wasn’t dropped.

A few minutes later the police arrived in an armoured van, two squad cars and a helicopter. Everybody at the party was arrested. Baby William went to live with a foster family in Swansea and Boris was allowed to stay with his Granny. The Pontypool Post ran the headline, “Michael Jackson Style Baby-dangling incident shocker.”

One day Mrs Richards who lived next door to his Granny said “I don’t believe in autism.” Boris replied, “My Dad said he doesn’t believe in the Royal Family, but I don’t know what that means because I saw the Queen on TV at Christmas.” When Boris’s mum found out, she went to Mrs Richards house and shouted at her for 25 minutes until she lost her voice.

When Boris turned fifteen he was allowed to stay with his parents at weekends. One weekend when he was watching TV, there was a knock on the door. Boris’s Dad opened it and Boris could hear the conversation.

"Hello, why do you have ladies tights over your head?" Boris heard his father say.

"You didn't return the money you borrowed so now you have to answer to Mr M," said a rasping voice.

"I spent the money on Sugar Puffs and fish food. Come back next week please," said Boris's Dad. Boris heard his Dad trying to close the door.

"Oh no you don't, you twit," said the bad voice.

Boris ran into the hall in time to see a tall man with a stocking over his head with holes cut out for his mouth and

eyes. He also noticed the man's trench coat and purple cravat. The attacker violently pushed the door open and grabbed Boris's Dad's wallet. He chased the attacker who jumped into a van and quickly drove away. Boris always remembered the van was yellow with "Moriarty Finance" written on the back door.

Later when Boris's Mum, Ivana Quatermaine, came home she yelled in her Russian accent, "Robert, I told you not to borrow money from zem."

Boris's Dad replied, "But I saw the advert on the telly when I was watching Bingo the Toxic Rabbit, and the lady looked really kind."

"I can't take any more of zis," said Ivana. For the rest of the evening she sat in the corner rocking back and forward singing a Russian lullaby.

The next day Boris's mother went completely mad and ran away from the house screaming like a maniac imagining there was a giant monkey-monster with wings chasing her. Boris never saw her again.

Angus Douglas Damien Gerry McCreedie

from Livingston in Scotland

CHAPTER TWO

MEET ANGUS

The second main character in my book is Angus Douglas Damien Gerry McCreedie. Angus lived in Livingston in Scotland for half of every year. The other half of each year the family relocated to a different country because of his Dad's job.

So every six months Angus asked, "Why do we have to move to a new rotten country every six stinking months Dad? I am afraid of new people."

"Because of my Job," his Dad replied. His Dad would then scratch his tummy and say, "Just pretend the new people you meet are people you already know."

When Angus met new people he felt compelled to do silly things that made no sense and annoyed him. He would walk forward, and then walk backward, and then walk forward again, like he was being controlled by a remote control and someone was pushing 'play', 'rewind', 'play'. Even thinking that he might meet a new person made him play, rewind and play. This was worse when walking through a door and someone was behind him.

When he was in Scotland Angus went bowling every Friday night with the Livingston Special Bus Club. Once his Dad said, "Come on Angus try harder, your score is lower than everyone else." When Angus looked confused his Dad pointed up at the TV set above the bowling lane, "See, your score is lower than the others, you need to hit more skittles. I don't think you are trying."

Angus replied, "but I like the cartoon it shows about the skittles when I miss."

Mr McCreedie scratched his fat tummy and said, "Ok, but if you hit the skittles then you can win. Pretend the skittles are the heads of your enemies, that'll help you bowl better."

"I don't have any enemies Dad," said Angus, "Do you?"

"Aye! I don't think Henry Jekyll likes me."

"Who is he?" said Angus.

"He is a scientist at work who stole my idea, and he is a bully," said Angus's Dad, patting his large stomach. Angus wasn't really listening.

Two weeks later the McCreedies moved to Portugal. Angus's brother Callum had an angry teacher at school who put him in detention on the day they moved, so he missed the flight. When he got home the house was rented out to a family from Poland so he had to sleep in the shed till his family came back to Scotland.

In Portugal it was sunny all day so Angus bought some sun glasses. He was scared of the new people, so his Dad stuck a picture of Bingo the Toxic Rabbit inside each lens. The new next-door neighbour came to their house and Angus got anxious so he put on his sunglasses. It looked like Bingo the Toxic Rabbit was talking which made him laugh. The Portuguese lady said, "stop laughing at my English." Angus thought he was in trouble so he ran to his bedroom. He ran forward, backward and forward again.

The next day another visitor came to their house in Portugal. Angus wore his sunglasses so didn't see the man's face.

“What are you doing here Henry? Come to steal more of my secret ideas?” Said Mr McCreedie.

“That wasn’t me, it was Eddie Hyde the other guy,” said the stranger in a rasping voice.

“Rubbish, you and Mr Hyde are the same person,” shouted Angus’s Dad.

“Looks like we all have our secrets. But enough of that! Give me the computer password,” said the stranger jumping towards Angus’s Dad.

“Not so fast you moron,” said Angus’s Dad slamming the door on the man’s hand. The sound reminded Angus of stepping on bubble wrap.

Angus heard the man yell and scream, “Next time Mr Hyde will come instead of me!”

Angus’s Dad shut the door and said, “Come on Angus, time for us to move back to Scotland.”

“But we haven’t stayed here for six months yet,” said Angus.

“A wee change of plan son, we need to get out of here,” replied his father.

“But does that man know where we live in Scotland Dad?” asked Angus.

“Good point son, and I know just the place for you be safe. I heard about a summer school for teens with your kind of disability Angus. Would you like to go to learn about Robotics, the same thing I work with?” said his father.

Loretta Pauleen O'Brien

from County Cork in Ireland

CHAPTER THREE

MEET LORETTA

Loretta Pauleen O'Brien was the youngest of seven children. Her family lived on a small island in Cork that was connected to the mainland by an old humpback bridge. Mr and Mrs O'Brien ran a local seafood restaurant called Pizza d'Illuminatti that made triangular pizzas.

Loretta's brothers caught the fish & crabs for the restaurant. Her parents made the pizza bread. Loretta's only sister, Roseanne was 10 years older than her and worked in Slovakia as an ape trainer for the International Rare Diseases Research Charity.

Each Thursday a lady called Ethelyn came to the O'Brien's house by the sea. Ethelyn rode a horse and brought an extra horse for Loretta. They rode on the beach for an hour or more. Ethelyn lent Loretta her iPod so Loretta could listen to her favourite band The Disillusioned Scarecrows.

One summer evening Loretta and Ethelyn decided to ride their horses up to the restaurant. They saw a man limping away from the restaurant back to his car with the registration "LJS 1." He had a knitted cap on with grey hair and dark glasses. He wore a cotton jumper and fingerless gloves. He shouted back at the restaurant, "You could at least taste my cooking before not hiring me. One of these days you will rue this decision!" Mr and Mrs O'Brien stood under the triangular Pizza D'illuminati's sign. Mr O'Brien's face was very white and he was shaking. Mrs O'Brien had tears in her eyes and was holding onto her husband.

Ethelyn looked as the man drove away and said, "This isn't a good time to see your Mum and Dad." Loretta looked at her watch and said, “Why is six-thirty-two a bad time to see them?”

“It doesn’t matter, let’s just go back to your house,” said Ethelyn.

That night Loretta ate her triangle pizza with calamari and lobster toppings. Mrs O’Brien had come home early from the restaurant and her eyes were red. “Mammy what’s wrong?” asked Loretta.

“Nothing, but I think you should call your older sister on Skype. She left a message for you,” said her mother.

Loretta asked, “Why?”

“I don’t know, she just left a message for you to call her,” said her mother.

Loretta went up to her parent’s bedroom and unplugged her tablet. Then she went into her own bedroom which had posters of The Disillusioned Scarecrows and Bingo the Toxic Rabbit on the walls. She sat on her bed and turned on the tablet, clicking on the ape picture, for her sister. A minute later she heard her sister’s voice and saw what looked like her own face: soft pale skin, blue eyes and a blond bob. But this wasn’t Loretta, it was Roseanne her sister in Slovakia.

“Hi Baby Sis!” said the smiling Roseanne wearing a white lab coat. Roseanne was at work in a large white room.

Loretta saw a medium-sized blackback gorilla which she recognised from her last skype.

“Is that Clyde?” asked Loretta.

“Spot on. He has been learning a lot. He’s very clever but he still can’t spell his own name,” answered Roseanne.

“Did you teach the ape to write?” asked Loretta in awe.

"No, just joking," said Roseanne.

"Oh," said Loretta, "I always miss jokes don't I?"

"Sorry, I shouldn't tell them, or I should tell you when it is a joke. Reggie the silverback you saw last time lost his banana privileges again," said Roseanne.

"Oh, is he still flinging his poo at the other gorillas?" asked Loretta.

"You guessed it! Anyway I am glad you called because I heard about something I think you would love. Some scientists I know are organising a summer school for kids with special needs, especially teenagers with autism. I told Mammy already and she says you can go if you want to. It's in Dublin in two weeks' time."

"I'm not sure. Is it about science?" asked Loretta.

"Yes, a scientist called Dr Chapeau de Guerre is running it. I think you would love it. It will be fun," said Roseanne.

"I'm not sure," replied Loretta biting her lip as she always did when she was anxious.

CHAPTER FOUR

DR CHAPEAU DE GUERRE'S INSTITUTE FOR SPECIAL ROBOTICS

Loretta decided to go to the summer school in Dublin. She was so bored that she fell asleep after an hour in the car. She dreamt about the man who shouted at her parents when he didn't get a job as the chef in their restaurant Pizza D'Illuminatti. In the dream, he was standing on an old wooden sailing ship looking out to sea and laughing. The car stopped suddenly and she woke up.

"Wake up my dear, we're here," Loretta heard her mother say.

"Of course we are here, but where is here?" answered Loretta.

"Why, Doctor Chapeau de Guerre's Institute for Special Robotics. I'll come in with you, in case you don't like any of the strangers," offered her mother.

"Look at this place Mammy. I've never seen a building like this on top of a hill in the countryside. It looks like an old army barracks," said Loretta as she pulled her bag out of the back of the car.

"Yes, this used to be the old army magazine fort, but we aren't in the countryside. We are right in the middle of Dublin, in the Phoenix Park," her mother explained.

Half an hour later, after picking up Loretta's name tag they went into an assembly hall and took seats. The hall had a stage at one end with steps leading up to it on either

The Phoenix Park

side. There were small windows high up on the walls that were grubby and let in very little light. Fluorescent tube lighting hung, flickering from the ceiling. Plastic bucket chairs stood in ten rows. The parents sat down at the back but Loretta wasn't worried. She sat at the front beside a boy about her own age and said, "Hi my name is Loretta O'Brien. What is your name?"

"My name is Boris Rhys Eli Ronald Quartermaine. I am from Pontypool in Wales. Have you ever heard of Bingo the Toxic Rabbit?" he said in a Welsh accent.

"I have heard of Bingo the Toxic Rabbit. He is my favourite cartoon character. I have a poster of him on my bedroom wall at home in Cork," replied Loretta.

The meeting had not started yet and people were still arriving. Boris and Loretta saw a tall, skinny boy wearing sun glasses. He was linking arms with a messy looking man with a round tummy wearing a wooly hat. The man pointed at the row Boris and Loretta were sitting in. The boy started walking towards them and then stopped, and stepped back a few steps then stepped forward again. He stopped and said "Hello Bingo, nice day isn't it."

"Yes it is, but why did you call me Bingo?" asked Boris.

"Oh, I'm sorry I am wearing special glasses that make strangers look like Bingo the Toxic Rabbit. I'm nervous with strangers. Can I pretend that you are my friends?" The tall boy asked.

"If you like Bingo the Toxic Rabbit then let's pretend we are best friends," said Boris.

"We love that cartoon. My name is Loretta O'Brien from Cork here in Ireland. This is Boris Rice Elephant Quaterpounder. He is from party something," said Loretta.

"No, no, no, no that's wrong. My real names is Boris Rhys Eli Ronald Quartermaine. I am from Pontypool in Wales," said Boris.

"Sorry Boris," said Loretta.

"Don't mention it," said Boris.

"My name is Angus Douglas Damien Gerry McCreedy. I am from Livingston in Scotland," said the tall boy.

"Hello Angus," said Loretta and Boris.

The three friends went quiet as Dr Chapeau de Guerre walked onto the stage. He was about sixty-nine years old, and had eagle eyes and a trench coat that was black. He had elf-like ears and wore an admiral's hat. He lowered his hat and when he spoke it sounded like he had a French accent.

"Welcome to my Institute for Special Robotics. I 'ope you 'ave all come 'ere safely and 'appily.

“First off, ze rules are, one: do not leave ze centre wizout permission.

“Two: don’t be mean to anyone because of zer skin colour; ‘air colour; race; gender; ethnicity; nationality; accent; religion; personality; facial features; appearance; eye colour; physical disability; intellectual disability; clothing; ‘eight; weight; eye wear; favourite pastimes; shoe size or nose shape or anyzing else!

Dr Chapeau de Guerre

from France

"Thirdly: you 'ave to be at your bedrooms at 11pm each night and classes start at 8 am each morning. Now it is time for ze parents to go. You may bid zem farewell. Students should be back in ze 'all in ten minutes," said Chapeau de Guerre.

Angus went over to his dad at the back of the hall and said, "Goodbye Dad."

"See you in two weeks Angus", said Mr Mcreedie. "It looks like you've made friends already. That's great."

"Yes Dad, but I am really worried that I might meet somebody I don't like," replied Angus. Mr McCreedie patted his tummy and waved as he walked out the door.

"Will you be OK Loretta dear?" said Mrs O'Brien in her soft voice.

"I think so Mammy. Can I call you on Skype?" Asked Loretta.

"I am sure you can, be good and have fun now," said Mrs O'Brien as she hugged her daughter, wiped a tear from her eye and left the hall.

"You can go now Father," said Boris.

"OK, Bye," said Mr Quatermaine stiffly turning around and walking out.

"Enough!" the kids heard a rasping female voice coming from a wrinkly scarecrow of a woman on the stage. "Your parents are gone, and you there stop your crying immediately," she said pointing at a black boy in a blue tracksuit who was sobbing.

Dr Chapeau de Guerre continued "Now I will introduce ze teachers. First, my deputy: Catriona Merryweather 'oo will teach Assistive Technology." He pointed at the angry scarecrow woman. A brown-haired lady with a hooked nose and cross-looking eyebrows stepped forward and snarled like a wolf.

"Secondly," went on Dr Chapeau de Guerre, "James Eckhart 'oo will teach Science Experiments with Toxic Waste." A grey-haired gentleman wearing a white lab coat with a moustache, whiskery chin and bushy eyebrows stepped forward and gave a short salute.

"Third, Humphrey Dunphy 'oo will teach Creativity." A taller, round man with a comb-over, wearing a tank top with zig-zag designs on it stepped forward and gave a thumb-up sign to the students.

"Lastly, Henry O'Doherty," continued Chapeau de Guerre making an effort to deliberately pronounce the H in Henry. "Henry is not a teacher, but will be your counsellor for zee summer school." A young man with blond hair and rectangle glasses wearing a beige shirt and tie stepped forward biting his nails and nodded his head at the students.

The students whispered to each other. Loretta said, “That Merrywheather lady looks like a scarecrow. I don’t really like her.”

Angus said, “Humphrey Dunphy looks like someone, but I don’t know who.”

“The principal looks like something out of a war film,” said Boris adding, “but nice hat though!”

Catriona Merryweather

a bit of a scarecrow

CHAPTER FIVE

CATRIONA MERRYWEATHER'S CLASS

The Assistive Technology class was held in a workshop. Unusual machines, shop dummies and wires covered the floor of the big room.

The teacher entered by slamming the door open and snarling. She marched over to the blackboard with her shoulders hunched and wrote her name in squiggly, hard-to-read handwriting.

"Hello everybody. My name is on the blackboard. Anyone who messes in this class will be sent to detention and get a bowling ball bounced on their head."

Angus put his hand up and asked, "Miss, are you really going to hit us on the head with a bowling ball?"

The teacher, Catriona Merryweather, forced a smile onto her purple bristly lips and said, “Eh... what I meant was... you won’t get pudding.”

“The purpose of this class is to help each of you get over your disabilities using robotics and cybernetic stuff. You will build a suit out of electrical equipment here in this workshop. It is up to you to design it and you can use anything you see,” she continued.

The black boy in the blue tracksuit stuck his hand up, and asked, “What does that mean?”

Merryweather looked at the boy and read his name from his badge, “Well Mr Tim Eckleston, if your legs don’t work properly and you normally go around in a wheel chair, you could build a cybernetic suit with robotic legs.”

Tim looked back and said, “I have ADHD, how can a suit make me concentrate better?”

Merryweather; her eyes bulging and bloodshot snapped back, “Don’t ask silly questions. Do I have to invent everything for you? Now get to work IMMEDIATELY!”

At the end of the class most students hadn’t got anything done. Some of them were day dreaming and others were playing with the equipment in a dangerous way. However Angus was figuring things out quite well. He, Boris and Loretta were working together in one corner. Angus was building a hover-robo-rabbit based on Bingo the Toxic Rabbit from TV.

Angus said, "Boris please find me the screwdriver so I can attach the ears to his head."

Loretta asked, "What are those buttons for Angus?"

Angus replied, "Those buttons control what he does, like going up and down, or fetching things from a cupboard. Ok let's test him."

Angus pressed the buttons. It started destroying everything, smashing windows and chairs. It whizzed round and round like a spinning-top gone mad.

Merryweather shouted, "Turn that thing off or you will all get detention."

"I forgot to make a remote control, I can't catch it to turn it off," said Angus running after it.

"Hold on I'll get it," said Boris, taking an apple from his pocket, aiming and throwing it at the robot as it raced around the room. BOOM, direct hit! Bingo the Toxic Rabbit blew into a million pieces.

"MR QUARTERMAINE, MR MCCREEDIE AND MISS O'BRIEN, I SENTENCE YOU TO DETENTION!" screamed Catriona Merryweather, her face red and crazy.

"Not the bowling ball!" said Angus squeezing his face in anxiety.

A boy wearing a light brown jacket with a traditional Indian style collar and square glasses danced for delight and laughed like there was no tomorrow.

"Stephen Micklewhite, you will be next, I am warning you!" growled Merryweather. Stephen went quiet but continued to giggle.

After the class, Angus was still holding his hands over his head to protect him from any bouncing bowling balls. "Don't worry Angus, teachers aren't allowed to hurt students," said Loretta.

"That robot you built was brilliant Angus. Where did you learn how to make cybernetic stuff?" asked Boris.

"That is my Dad's job," answered Angus, "sometimes he brings broken robots home and he shows me how to fix them."

"Do you think you could make me a high-tech jacket?" asked Boris. He explained that he didn't like people touching him and wanted something special to keep people away.

"Hmm, I don't know," said Angus.

"Maybe you could make a jacket that gives people an electric shock if they touch you," suggested Loretta.

"Brilliant idea," said Boris.

"Let's make one next class," said Angus.

Humphrey Dunphy

CHAPTER SIX

HUMPHREY DUNPHY'S CLASS

In Humphrey Dunphy's class the students were encouraged to make up stories, to help them think up new creative ideas.

The classroom had lots of couches to sit on and the walls were covered in posters from different TV shows, movies and books to inspire the students. There were also computers, typewriters, pens and paper on tables.

Mr Dunphy spoke to the class standing beside Tim Eckleston. His voice was high pitched and squeaky, "Hello everybody, my name is Humphrey Dunphy. New students should know that we all are good at making stories and by the way we already have an author in our class. I want you to give a warm round of applause to Tim Eckleston who is writing his first book, "Goodbye Happiness, Hooray for Nothing." (See the back of this book.)

The class clapped for a minute and then the teacher continued, "It is a book of short stories involving tragedies from different places in the world."

"What does that even mean?" whispered Boris to Loretta and Angus.

Stephen Micklewhite put his hand up and said, "I have a good poem. Humphrey Dunphy sat on a wall, Humphrey

Tim Eckleston

Dunphy had a great fall." Stephen burst into laughter like a hyena thumping his hand on Boris's back.

Boris jumped up and slapped Stephen, shouting, "Don't touch me or I'll put marmite on you and get a dog to chase you."

Stephen stopped laughing and said, "yeah right."

Mr Dunphy stepped forward and said, "Is everyone being nice to each other? Ok please find a piece of paper and a pen and start writing the first thing that comes into your head."

The three friends went to sit at a table together. Loretta asked Boris, "Are you ok Boris?"

Boris answered, "That just gave me an idea about Bingo the Toxic Rabbit. Remember that time on TV, after Bingo was accidently super-charged with particle radiation and a bad guy hit him. The baddie was instantly turned into a pile of nuclear fall-out dust. Angus can you make a suit that can do that to Stephen Micklewhite?"

"I think that's going a bit too far Boris," said Loretta.

"But Loretta, what if a strange guy comes to me with a knife? Actually, one time a guy came to my house and stole my Dad's wallet. If I had a bazooka or something, then I could kill the man," said Boris.

"I don't think that's a good idea Boris, we shouldn't kill. What would our parents say?" said Loretta, biting her lip.

“I don’t know what my Mum would say because she ran away,” said Boris.

“Well my Mammy would say it’s wrong. If we’re going to make suits then we need to make them friendly to other people, not violent,” said Loretta.

“That’s for sure. That should be our policy,” said Angus. Boris looked like he wasn’t convinced.

Angus continued, “If you agree to this code Boris, then I will make you a suit that will stop people touching you.”

”I want the suit to have a flame thrower, then I’ll agree,” said Boris.

“No Boris, no flame thrower! How about a net to catch baddies?” suggested Loretta.

“That would be good I think,” said Angus.

“That’s a good idea. I could catch the man who stole my Dad’s wallet. Instead of killing him I could bring him to the police!” said Boris.

“Let’s shake on it,” said Loretta, then looking at Boris she remembered and said, “or not shake, let’s put thumbs up if you agree.”

They all put their thumbs up and smiled.

“Did you think of a story?” asked the teacher who had walked over to their table.

“No, but we have an idea of how to catch criminals,” Said Boris.

“That sounds like the start of a great story. I love crime novels,” said Mr Dunphy.

Professor James Eckhart

from Belfast in Northern Ireland

CHAPTER SEVEN

JAMES ECKHART'S CLASS

"Before you come into my classroom, you should put on your safety goggles, hair nets, gloves and white coats," said James Eckhart. He led them into a room like a tour guide. In the room, all the safety clothing was hanging up. Each student got ready and followed Professor Eckhart into the laboratory.

Angus put his hand up and asked, "Why do we have to wear this protective clothing?"

"Good question. We wear the clothes because we might get exposed to radiation or poisonous gases and liquids. There is a risk of turning into toxic-waste-contaminated-beasts, for example changing species because the chemicals are mixed with animal fur," said the professor.

A boy named Maurice Humphreys said, "Yeah, careful Gerald, you might turn into a human if you are not careful."

His friend Gerald Macintosh replied, "But I am a human."

"I thought you were a werewolf, look at your long hair and big furry monobrow," said Maurice.

Professor Eckhart cleared his throat and said, "Maurice, let's get back to the topic shall we? OK here on the wall are some instructions for mixing chemicals. Also you can check on that computer over there for more information. Mix them in the beakers and test tubes on that shelf. We won't test our experiments on people or animals; we will use the plants at the back of the room. I want you to invent a mixture to make a plant move or turn it into something else. Ask me if you need help."

Maurice and Gerald were working at a table together. Maurice was using tweezers to take out some of Gerald's eyebrows. They were trying to make werewolf daffodils.

The teacher put Stephen Michelwhite and Tim Eckleston at a desk together. Stephen poured a beaker of green goo on Tim's head and roared laughing as it started to sizzle. James Eckhart rushed over and started scraping off the goo before it burnt off all of Tim's hair. "Stephen I don't want you to play with these chemicals, it is not playdough," said the professor.

"You look like a monk!" laughed Stephen pointing at a bald patch on Tim's head.

"That's not funny. My mum will be cross with you now. I don't want to be a monk," cried poor Tim.

"The best of men get tonsures Tim, look at me," said James Eckhart, comforting him by showing him his bald patch on the back of his head.

Angus put his hand up again and asked, "How can we use toxic waste to build robotic stuff?"

"Have you heard of mutated cyborg creatures?" asked Eckhart.

Angus, Boris and Loretta all said, "No."

Eckhart explained, "We won't be doing it in this summer school because it is very advanced. But there is a book about it behind you on that shelf."

Loretta stretched and took down the large book. Then she said, "This book is written by James Eckhart, is this your book Professor?"

"Yes, it's a collection of what I learned over the years about toxic waste," replied Eckhart.

Professor Eckhart sat at their table for the rest of the class. He asked them all about themselves, their lives and favourite things.

After the class as they headed to their bedrooms. Angus said to Loretta and Boris, “He is a very nice man. I think he is the best teacher I have had.”

“I am unable to think. I feel too tired to walk. I am almost dizzy. I need to go to bed”, said Loretta.

“I think you should Skype home like you said you would,” said Boris.

“Yes I think so, but then I really need to sleep,” said Loretta.

“I hope they don’t have a bowling ball in detention”, said Angus.

“I don’t think they will use one Angus,” said Boris, “Don’t be worried, just keep thinking about building a suit for me.”

“I think I will ask James Eckhart to talk to Catriona Merryweather just in case,” said Angus turning back towards the class room.

The League of

Conveniently Out-of-Copyright Villains

CHAPTER EIGHT

THE LEAGUE OF CONVENIENTLY OUT-OF-COPYRIGHT VILLAINS

Angus went looking for James Eckhart but couldn't find him. The laboratory was locked so he went to the staff room which was close by. He opened the door a little but stopped when he heard people talking. He didn't go in fully because he didn't want to get in trouble with Catriona Merryweather and he could hear her saying something.

"These students will make perfect guinea-pigs for our experiments. It was a great idea to pretend to run a summer school. I thought kidnapping kids was the only way to do it," said Merryweather's voice, purring like a tiger.

"Why would we do zat when we can get zem to come 'ere voluntarily? We didn't even 'ave to organise transport. Zer parents brought zem 'ere," said Doctor Chapeau de Guerre in his French accent laughing.

"I don't think this is a good idea Doctor Chapeau de Guerre. These are special-needs children for Pete's sake!" Angus knew that was James Eckhart's mild Belfast accent.

"If you don't agree with us zen I will never release your brother," said Chapeau de Guerre in a booming voice.

"I know about my brother, but this isn't just about him. I am not sure if the experiments will work on these kids. Something might go terribly wrong. We tested on animals before, but humans are different. We need more time," said Eckhart.

"Volgen says we 'ave to do zis now!" shouted Chapeau de Guerre. "And you know why this will only work with zees kids. In cybernetics, special-needs mean special powers. Anyway enough of zat talk. Henry O'Doherty as summer school counsellor; are you ready to hypnotise all zee students tomorrow? And just remember, we 'ave your Dad under our control in case you are 'aving second thoughts. You 'ave made a deal and zat is final."

Angus didn't understand what they were talking about but he knew what hypnotising people meant and felt extra worried. He heard Henry O'Doherty answer with a nervous stutter, "Yes, sir, I- I- I,'ll have them all under control soon enough, please j- j- just let me know what characters you want them to believe they are."

"Good question Henry. Anybody 'ave any ideas? We seem to be running out of villains from books to turn our victims into. It really 'elps zem get into character as a baddie if zey know zee book or film," said Chapeau de Guerre.

"Why not just use villains from new books Doctor?" asked Humphrey Dunphy. "There is a book about a boy wizard who has to fight a really brilliant evil dark wizard called..."

"DO NOT SAY HIS NAME! No we always run into copyright issues with villains from new books. It is much more convenient to stick to old books. Ok, let's all think of somezing before tomorrow," said Chapeau de Guerre. "Talking about our villains, where are zey?"

Angus was frozen with fear. He peaked in through the door and saw another door open on the other side of the room. In walked some mean looking people. One had a limp and a parrot on his shoulder. Another was wearing a purple cravat. A third had a patch over his eye and looked like Captain Hook from Peter Pan. A lady with green skin wore a witch's hat.

They all sat down around a large table with Chapeau de Guerre at the top, wearing his admiral's hat.

"Welcome everyone to zee league of Conveniently Out-of-Copyright Villains. Ok ok, so 'oo was meant to bring zee refreshing beverages and sandwiches?" asked Chapeau de Guerre.

Everyone stayed quiet and looked away from Chapeau de Guerre.

"Well zis is a bad start. 'ow can we take over zee world if we don't have refreshments for our meetings? Do our roll call please number two," said Chapeau de Guerre.

Catriona Merryweather took a clip board out and started to call the names.

"Doctor Chapeau de Guerre." "'ere."

"Humphrey Dunphy." "Here."

"James Eckhart." "Here."

"Henry O'Doherty." "H-H-Here."

"Long John Silver." "Aye."

"Count Dracula." "Here."

"Doctor Jekyll and Mr Hyde." "Both Here."

"Captain James Hook." "Aye."

"The Wicked Witch of the West." "Here my pretty."

"Professor Moriarty." "Here."

"Ok, where is zee speaking stick? Then, whoever has zee stick can take zeir turn to speak," asked Chapeau de Guerre sounding frustrated.

"I have it right here in me pocket. And I have a word I'd like to say, beggin' yer pardon Doctor Boss," said a man in a pirate accent. Angus heard a parrot squawk.

"Very well, Long John Silver, do you want to go first?" said Chapeau de Guerre's voice again.

"That I do Boss. Don't mean to be complainin', but I was the pirate around here for years. Why did we need another one?" asked Silver.

Professor Moriarty and Count Dracula

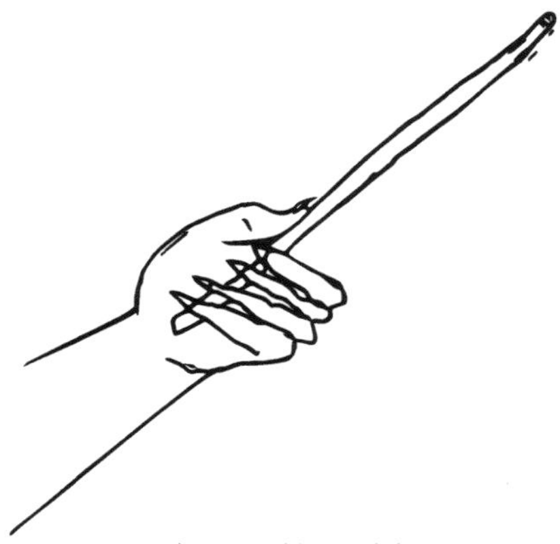

The Speaking Stick

In answer, Angus heard a familiar voice say, “If it wasn’t for the cursed Peter Pan I’d be sailing the Jolly Roger back in Never Land.”

Then Humphrey Dunphy whispered loudly in his high pitched voice, “Isn’t the Peter Pan book still in copyright?”

“Enough!” shouted Chapeau de Guerre again. “Two pirates are better zan one. You both make very scary villains.” Then in a whisper, “And no Humphrey, zee details are complicated but for most purposes Peter Pan entered zee public domain in 2008.”

“If two pirates are better than one, I say why not have three? Where is me trusted side-kick Mr Smee?” asked Captain Hook.

“Oh yes, I remember Mr Smee,” said Chapeau de Guerre, “Actually I think ‘e will be back tomorrow. Henry, put zat name top of your list.”

“Silver, please pass the speaking stick to Doctor Jekyll, or is it Mr Hyde today perhaps,” said Chapeau de Guerre.

“Just Henry Jekyll today,” said a voice that Angus remembered from his trip to Portugal with his father.

Doctor Jekyll… or is it Mr Hyde?

“I tried to get the computer password like you told me Boss, I even tracked McCreedie down to Portugal where he was hiding. But he slammed the door on my arm,” said Jekyll.

“Zis is not good enough! If we don’t get zat computer password we can’t see zee secret plans McCreedie designed for a super robot-drone. You should ‘ave turned into Mr Hyde and bashed zee door down. Anyway it doesn’t matter now because we ‘ave ‘is son ‘ere, we can use ‘im as an ‘ostage,” said Chapeau de Guerre.

Angus wet his pants with fear. He ran off quietly to tell Loretta and Boris. He ran forward, backward and forward again.

CHAPTER NINE

RUN!

Angus ran up the stairs terrified that something awful would happen, such as a bowling ball dropping on his head like a basketball falling through a hoop. He felt the urge to step backwards down two steps and then continue up the steps. His brain always seemed to tell him to 'play-reverse-play' to stop bad things happening to him. He knew it was illogical but that is the way he saw things.

At the top of the stairs he met Loretta.

"Where are you going Angus?" she said.

"Loretta... I think that something, oh I don't know how to say it all," said Angus.

"Why do you always go forward, backward and forward again Angus?" asked Loretta.

"It's to stop bad things happening. I know it doesn't make sense but I feel compelled to do it. I think it is OCD," answered Angus. "But that isn't the thing. I don't think this is a summer-school. This is a place for special robotics where they hypnotise children to turn them into minions of Doctor Chapeau de Guerre. We need to get out of here quick."

"Emm... let's get Boris. And I should Skype home. Oh, I see you need to change your trousers. Meet me in my room in five minutes," said Loretta.

Five minutes later Angus came into Loretta's bedroom. Boris was sitting on the bed beside Loretta. They were talking on Loretta's tablet to someone.

"That's surprising, what are you doing back home in Cork, Roseanne?" said Loretta.

"Your sister lost her job in Slovakia Loretta," said a soft voice that was Loretta's mother. "I see you have friends there."

"Yes this is my friend Boris Roast Elf Quatermaster from Pointy-Pen in Wales," said Loretta.

"No No, wrong again, I am Boris Rhys Eli Ronald Quatermaine, from Pontypool in Wales," corrected Boris.

"Sorry Boris," said Loretta.

"Don't mention it," said Boris.

"And Angus is here from Scotland," added Boris.

"Hello boys," said a girl on the tablet who looked like an older version of Loretta.

"But Roseanne, what happened to the gorillas and your job?" Asked Loretta.

"It's a long story, but the International Rare Diseases Research Charity closed down the whole lab. The whole thing was a sham. Apparently training apes has nothing to do with rare disease research. I was such an eejit. They tricked me into the job because they knew I loved our primate cousins. They really only wanted to get information about the Illuminati," said Roseanne who looked like she had been crying.

"It's OK Roseanne, sure we could buy you a little pet monkey if possible," said her mother.

"Why did they want to spy on our Pizza restaurant?" asked Loretta.

"Well, it wasn't the Pizza they wanted to know about. They think your father is part of a secret organisation called the Illuminati," said Mrs O'Brien.

"Is he?" asked Loretta.

"No of course not. Sure it's just the name of the Pizza restaurant," said Roseanne.

“But that didn’t stop them giving you a fake job and sending that pirate-like guy to work here, all just to spy on us,” said Mrs O’Brien.

“Jings Cribbens. Did that pirate have a limp and a knitted hat?” asked Angus kneeling on the bed behind Loretta and Boris.

“Indeed he did,” said Mrs O’Brien

“He’s here! He’s a hypnotised minion of Dr Chapeau de Guerre. He also has Captain Hook, Dracula and other bad people from story books. He even has the Wicked Witch of the West,” cried Angus whose face was pale with fright.

“What a load of baloney!” said Boris.

“It’s true. They want special-needs-kids to become brain-washed baddies from famous old books. They want to do perilous experiments on us to mutate us into bio-cyber-criminals. Here I can show you the room downstairs where they are talking,” said Angus.

Angus led Loretta and Boris downstairs. Loretta was still holding the tablet and she whispered for her mammy and sister to be quiet. Angus had a worried feeling in his tummy and tiptoed towards the staff room. He reversed a few times and bumped into the others.

As they turned a corner they froze in silence. Right ahead of them they saw the horrible visage of Dracula with hair combed back from a widow's peak, and pointy triangular fangs.

Angus screamed like a little girl and turned, bumping into the other two. The three ran down the corridor dashed into the first room, and locked the door.

CHAPTER TEN

ECKHART'S LAB AND HYPNOSIS

"I know this place. It's Eckhart's lab," said Boris.

A voice came out of Loretta's tablet, "Where are you? What's happening?"

"We've run into James Eckhart's lab. He taught us about toxic waste. We were chased by Count Dracula. Mammy I'm frightened," answered Loretta.

"We're coming in the car right now to collect you. Stay where you are and don't do anything silly," said Loretta's Mother.

"I'll get some ideas from one of the books over here. You two lean against the door in case they find a key," said Boris running over to the book case.

Boris spotted something in one of the books. He saw a picture of a dragon breathing fire. The toxic recipe was called 'Dragon Flames'. He started finding the different bottles and mixed them up in a vial.

"Don't drink that Boris, it's poison!" said Loretta.

"But the book told me to do it," said Boris who immediately gulped it all down.

Boris bent over as if he was going to be sick. Loretta went over and put her hand on his back. "Don't touch me," he choked. Loretta backed away.

"Let's stay in here till... oh I don't know... till the rest of our lives," said Angus holding his hands over his head anxiously.

Loretta took out her tablet and started touching the screen. "It will take two hours and forty-nine minutes for my family to get here from Cork", said Loretta, "let's stay in the lab till they arrive."

The clock on the wall was taking its time. Boris crouched over with one hand against the wall the other hand thumping at his stomach in pain. Angus was pacing the room. Loretta was playing games on her tablet to pass the time.

They must have fallen asleep because the next thing Angus knew he was dreaming about Bingo the Toxic Rabbit. Bingo said "Angus, Angus!" But it wasn't Bingo, it was Professor James Eckhart.

"What are you all doing in my classroom? You are too early for class. It's time for you all to go to assembly with Doctor Chapeau de Guerre," said Eckhart.

In assembly, Doctor Chapeau de Guerre stood on the stage with his Admiral's hat looking very annoyed and tired. "According to what I 'eard, zer have been some students 'oo 'aven't been in zer beds on time last night. Zis was one of my main rules and words cannot describe 'ow disappointed I am."

"I think they are talking about us," whispered Angus to Loretta. Boris wasn't listening; he was rubbing his chest, still uncomfortable.

"But enough of zat!" continued Chapeau de Guerre. "Now Henry O'Doherty wants to talk to all of you students one by one. We will do it in alphabetical order, first Eckleston, Tim", Chapeau de Guerre pointed at a door.

"Please don't laugh at me", said Tim in his London accent. Stephen Micklewhite shrieked with laughter, pointing at Tim's bald spot where his hair had been burned away by the green goo the day before. Stephen laughed so much he fell off his chair.

Tim disappeared into the room. Five minutes later the door opened and Henry O'Doherty popped his head out and said, "H -H-Humphreys, Maurice".

Maurice stood up. He was easy to spot as he had no eyebrows; large, saucer-like eyes, and a thin nose with a little bit of moustache. He went into the room with Henry.

Angus whispered to Loretta, “I have an idea, can the three of us go outside for a bit?”

Henry O’Doherty

Boris burped and next thing Gerald Macintosh who was sitting in front of him said, “Is somebody burning toast?” Loretta noticed that Gerald’s hair was on fire. She put her coat over his head.

“Who turned out the lights?” cried Gerald.

“Sorry your hair was on fire Gerald,” said Loretta.

“Excuse me Professor Eckhart, can we take Boris out, he is feeling a bit, um, fired up,” said Loretta.

“Okay,” said Eckart.

Loretta took Boris by the shirt and left. Angus followed them.

CHAPTER ELEVEN

NEW BINGO, NEW VILLAINS

"Not that way, follow me to Catriona Merryweather's class," said Angus.

"I'll keep a look-out in case she comes back. I wonder where my family are, they should have been here hours ago," said Loretta.

"I need to go to the toilet," said Boris who looked ill.

Inside the classroom Angus started searching for equipment and parts. Soon there was a pile of stuff on the table including many coloured wires, light bulbs, pieces of metal, batteries, computer chips, propellers, and loads of nuts and bolts.

Angus worked fast. He saved time by taping bits together with duct tape instead of gluing or welding them. He used a round vacuum cleaner for the main body. The wheels were from a shopping trolley. Bingo's face was drawn on in black marker. He bent old clothes hangers into bunny-ear shapes and attached them to the top as antennae for the remote control.

"Loretta, can I use your tablet for a remote-control?" asked Angus.

Loretta handed it over, "Yes of course, here."

Angus downloaded a universal remote-control app and started testing.

They heard a 'kaboom' noise in the coridor and then Boris came back from the toilet looking very red in the face. "I thought I was going to puke, but I just let out a huge burp and set the bathroom on fire. The toilet exploded and the hand dryer machine melted."

"Do you feel ok Boris?" asked Loretta.

"I feel super. I think I am a dragon, a real Welsh dragon!" answered Boris. "What is Angus doing?"

"Oh, I think he is building a new Bingo robot. This time he has a remote control," answered Loretta.

"Have you weaponised it?" asked Boris, walking over to the table where Angus was concentrating on Loretta's tablet pressing the screen. Lights flashed on and off on the robot.

"Er, well sometimes it electrocutes you if you touch his ears, but that was a mistake because I wired it wrong. I also reversed the vacuum from suck to blow. The primary weapon is that it can fire carrots." Angus said.

"You know carrots are not going to defeat those villains Angus," Boris said.

"How about exploding carrots?" asked Angus.

"Good thinking," said Boris

"No, we can't kill people, boys. Normal carrots will have to do," added Loretta.

Weaponised Bingo the Toxic Rabit Robot

Suddenly the door burst open and Catriona Merryweather yelled, “Who said you could come into my classroom? Get back into the main hall now!”

Luckily Angus had put the robot on the ground to test it, and the teacher did not see it. Angus hid the tablet behind his back. They were marched back to the hall which was now empty.

Angus’s face looked white with fear as Merryweather said he was next to see the school counsellor Henry O’Doherty. She held his arm and marched him to the door. Angus stepped back several times which sent chairs crashing over and Merryweather into a rage.

“You stupid boy,” she screamed pushing him into the room, her hair wild and scraggily.

The last thing he saw before the door closed was Loretta in tears and Boris looking very red in the face.

“C-Calm down Angus, have a seat. It’s just you and me now,” said O’Doherty.

Angus sat down on a chair directly in front of O’Doherty and held his hands over his head. He started to cry and had wet himself a little bit.

“Ok, so let’s get started. Look into my eyes Angus, and relax. W-When I click my fingers, you will be Fu Manchu,” said O’Doherty.

"I don't like strangers, I have to wear my glasses or I will be too anxious," said Angus.

"Whatever, just relax," said O'Doherty.

Angus put on his sunglasses and saw Bingo the Toxic Rabbit's head on Henry O'Doherty's shoulders. He started to laugh.

"That's it, laughing is good. Now look into my eyes. You are Fu Manchu," said the counsellor in a quiet and slow voice.

"And you are a Rabbit. By the way, what is Fu Manchu?" asked Angus.

"No, this is going wrong. You are the controversial racial stereotype super villain Fu Manchu – the evil warlord. You will obey Doctor Chapeau de Guerre."

"What the heck do you mean?" responded Angus.

"Oh this is no good, you probably have never heard of Fu Manchu. I told them we had run out of well known out-of-copy-right-villains. Just a minute I will check the list to see which other characters are not used yet," said Henry O'Doherty reading from the clip board he was holding.

Outside the door an alarm went off and Merryweather charged into the room. Behind her Angus saw flames leaping and dancing in the hall. He took his glasses off and cried, "My friends!"

"Aren't you finished with him? Quick we need to leave and go to the main part of the plan!" shouted Merryweather.

Angus and O'Doherty were pushed through a door at the other end of the office. They entered a corridor with seats against the walls. On the seats were all of the villains Angus had seen the night before with new ones added. He could see Gerald Macintosh howling like a werewolf. Tim Ecclestone was dressed as a monk or something. Angus was frozen with fear as everyone looked at him.

"Don't tell me you 'aven't hypnotised 'im," said Chapeau de Guerre.

Henry O'Doherty looked flustered then patted Angus on the back and said, "Everyone, meet the newest m-member of the League of C-Conveniently Out-of-Copyright Villains," he paused, bit his lip for a moment then continued, "Captain, er... Scotland, or Lord Edinburgh."

"What book is Captain Scotland or Lord Edinburgh from Henry?" asked Chapeau de Guerre suspiciously.

O'Doherty bit his lip again and stuttered, "Er, from the well known b-book called," he paused to cough and continued saying each word slowly, "Horrible Scottish Nightmares about G-Ghosts and stuff. It's quite an old book, from a long time ago. You might not have heard of it."

Chapeau de Guerre looked puzzled but Merryweather interrupted her face red with fury and wickedness, “No time for this, the building is on fire we have to get out now!”

Chapeau de Guerre led the way out of the Magazine Fort and down the side of the hill followed by all the characters and staff. It was a steep hill and some of them tripped and rolled down. At the bottom of the hill Chapeau de Guerre called out, “Now our plan comes to the interesting bit. We will kidnap ze President”. Everyone cheered, apart from Angus, but nobody noticed.

“Zee easiest way to sneak into ze President’s ‘ouse is through ze Zoo. Ze army guard all ze gates, but Dublin Zoo is next door. We will go into ze Zoo and climb over ze fence into ze President’s back-garden. Zen nobody can stop us!”

Chapeau de Guerre put on his Admirals hat and stuck his hand inside his jacket like Napoleon his distant ancestor and off he marched. All the villains followed him. Angus looked back trying to see his friends. The fort was in flames.

CHAPTER TWELVE

CHASE THROUGH THE PARK

Nearly all the fort was on fire. Boris and Loretta climbed out through a window and made their way down the hill holding a long curtain as a rope.

"Oh no, we forgot Bingo," said Boris.

"I'll turn this thing on to see if the remote control works from here. Then I really need to call my parents," Said Loretta.

Loretta pressed the tablet screen a few times but nothing seemed to happen. Boris and Loretta looked up at the Magazine Fort but there was no sign of the robot. Then suddenly from the flames a fireball shot out and rolled down the hill towards them. They jumped out of the way just in time.

"What was that? Oh look it's Bingo. He made it, but he's melted a bit," said Boris running over.

Loretta continued to press the screen of her tablet and soon she saw her sister's face.

"I'm so sorry we didn't rescue you Loretta. I hope you are ok. The Magazine Fort was locked shut and we couldn't get in," said Roseanne.

"Where are you now?" asked Loretta.

"We are here in the Phoenix Park. We have the van hidden in bushes by the cricket ground, across from the Zoo. Hold on Loretta I see something. There's a bunch of weirdos marching over this way through the fields. The leader is wearing an old admiral's hat. One of the ladies has green skin. There is a guy who looks like a vampire," whispered Roseanne.

"That's them. Keep quiet Roseanne", Loretta heard her mother say on the tablet.

"Do they have Angus?" asked Boris, who was listening in on the conversation.

Roseanne held her phone so that the camera pointed to the group walking past them. Boris and Loretta could see the villains walking along.

"I see Dracula; I see a werewolf who looks like Gerald; there is Humphrey Dunphy the tall overweight teacher," said Boris.

"I see him, there is Angus with that Merryweather woman holding his arm," said Loretta.

"They are going over the road to the Zoo," said Roseanne's voice.

"We have to rescue Angus," said Boris.

"Quick Roseanne call the Gardaí," they heard Loretta's mother cry.

"Ok, we will meet you by the Zoo gate in five minutes," said Roseanne. She hung up the call and the screen of the tablet went blank again.

"How do we get to the Zoo?" asked Boris.

"I think this path goes to the main road, then we can ask directions," said Loretta.

They had to roll Bingo down the rest of the hill to the road. Then once the surface was flat Bingo was able to drive along on his wheels. It was slow going as the road looked very long.

"You climb on the front and steer with your tablet and I will hold onto the back," said Boris.

Loretta sat on top of Bingo facing forwards and Boris sat the opposite way facing backwards. They had to bend the coat-hanger bunny ears sideways out of the way. The robot was quite slow with both of them riding him. After a long while they were on the main park road and saw a sign for the Zoo. This road was very long.

"This is taking ages. Hold on tight I have something that will speed us up," said Boris.

Loretta heard a loud belching sound behind her and nearly slipped backwards off the robot as it accelerated forward at an alarming pace. A few more fiery burps got them there in no time at all. She saw joggers and families walking along pointing at them and looking with their mouths open in wonder.

Loretta and Boris ridding a vacuum cleaner at top speed

The cricketers stopped their game to watch all the strange people going past. It looked like a fancy-dress party had just stopped the traffic to walk across the main park road to go to the Zoo. Then they saw two teenagers ridding a vacuum cleaner at top speed skidding to a halt beside the Ice-Cream van outside the Zoo gates. Next thing a van drove out of a large bush. It had Pizza D'Illuminati written on the side. It bumped over the grass and crossed the road driving up onto the path on the other side scattering pedestrians. An older couple jumped out of the van followed by a young blonde woman. All these people were heading into the Zoo. Some of the cricketers followed to see what was happening.

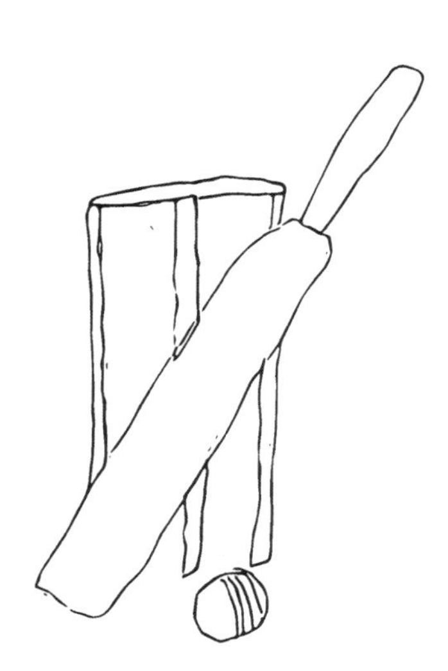

CHAPTER THIRTEEN

THE BATTLE OF DUBLIN ZOOLOGICAL GARDENS

"For Pete's sake, why are we paying to enter?" snapped Catriona Merryweather, her eyebrows a knot of spite and lunacy. The League of Conveniently Out-of-Copyright Villains, the teachers and a frightened Angus were all queuing at the Zoo gate behind Doctor Chapeau de Guerre who was talking to a lady behind a glass window with an opening at the bottom.

"Don't worry my dear, I will remember my PIN number any minute now, hmm, ah yes," said Chapeau de Guerre who then punched buttons on the credit card machine and handed it back to the lady through the opening.

"One more question, which part of ze Zoo is closest to ze President's back garden?" asked Chapeau de Guerre.

"African Plains I think. Feeding times for the Sumatran Tigers in 15 minutes," replied the lady.

Soon all the villains had got into the Zoo. Chapeau de Guerre held up the tri-fold map he got with the tickets. Everyone waited till he dramatically pointed the way to go. They marched after him as he limped off as fast as he could go. Some people laughed and pointed at them. A girl cried and hid behind her mother.

At that moment Boris and Loretta's family came through the gates after them. Loretta's mother told the manager of the Zoo that the fancy-dress-freaks were really dangerous-types and had a terrible conspiracy to capture the President of Ireland and overthrow worldwide freedom. The manager of the Zoo said if they could be stopped there would be a reward: free Zoo entry for the rest of their natural lives plus a two week holiday in Italy, courtesy of his sister Barbara who worked in a travel shop in the Jervis shopping centre.

Boris saw his friend Angus being dragged along by that terrible Merryweather creature. She was pulling him by the leg and he clawed at the ground trying to stop. He was crying and his trousers were ripped at both knees. His fingers were bloody.

The whole Zoo stopped as Boris roared. It wasn't a burp this time, but a real dragon-style noise that sounded like a football crowd cheering. The flames set trees and bushes on fire. He yelled and ran to save his friend. Loretta and her family followed. Loretta was controlling Bingo the Robot and she made it shoot off ahead of them.

“They are heading over to the City Farm, after them quick,” said Loretta’s sister Rosenne.

Merryweather croacked at Chapeau de Guerre, “Stop, we have to fight the heart-burn kid and the illuminati family.”

Doctor Chapeau de Guerre lined up the villains and teachers in the picnic area beside the City Farm and Reptile house. “Wait for my order,” he called with his hand in the air. Families scattered everywhere. Children hid in the Rabbit house. One granny climbed over the fence into the goat pen.

Then Boris appeared racing up the hill. To Chapeau de Guerre and the villains he looked like an angry teenager whose skin was a mixture of acne and red scales. He wore a red t-shirt.

“What is zat?”asked Chapeau de Guerre, “Is it a red dragon?”

“That red dragon is my friend,” said Angus.

**PARENTAL WARNING:
THE FOLLOWING PAGES HAVE
BEEN CLASSIFIED AS HORRIFIC
FOR YOUNGER READERS**

Chapeau de Guerre yelled, "ATTACK!" and his troops charged at Boris who kept running at them as fast as he could with his teeth gritted in a constipated fashion.

Loretta showed her Mum how to use the controls for the Robot. Mrs O'Brien climbed up a tree and spent the whole battle there directing Bingo the Robot remotely. Loretta saw a horse in the City Farm and knew what she needed to do. The cricket team and zoo keepers joined the goodies using cricket bats to whack the baddies. Roseanne, Loretta's big sister ran off saying, "I have an idea, I'll be back soon."

The fighting was fierce. Not many of them had weapons so mostly people were punching and kicking and biting. Merryweather growled like a wild animal and wrestled four zoo keepers at the same time. Long John Silver was duelling with Professor Eckhart who had joined the goodies. Silver had a sword and Eckhart used a parasol from a picnic table.

Professor Eckhart duels with Long John Silver

Loretta was charging back and forth on a horse knocking baddies over like skittles. Angus winced at the sound of crunching bones and squeals of pain all around him.

The scene is too violent to describe in a book aimed at older children and young adults. Certainly a movie version would be at least 16 cert. To summarise; Roseanne returned with an army of gorillas and other primates that obeyed her every word, they roared like warriors as they charged at Chapeau de Guerre's army. Dublin Zoo had bought the apes from the International Rare Disease Research Charity in Slovakia so the animals knew her well. Reggie had the time of his life tossing his poo at everyone.

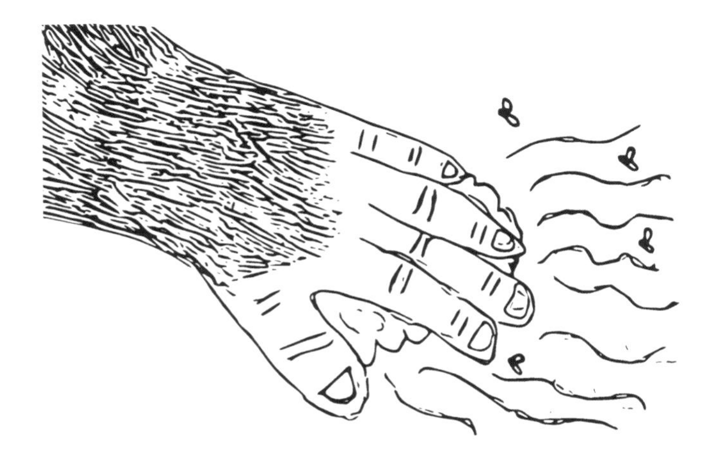

Reggie the ape flinging his poo

Boris, now known as the Red Dragon used his dragon powers to set most of the teachers on fire. They only survived by diving into the lake where they were attacked by flamingos.

Bingo the Robot's batteries ran out after an hour, but had managed to cause lots of damage, electrocuting villains left and right.

Angus, now known as "Captain Scotland or Lord Edinburgh" found his courage and joined the battle. He gave Humphrey Dunphy a wedgie, two Chinese burns and a poke in the eye. When Merryweather produced a bowling ball out of her backpack and shouted, "Death by bowling ball!" Angus quickly wrestled the ball from her grasp. It slipped out of his hands, flew briefly through the air, and landed with a crunch on the wicked teacher's fiendish face. She staggered away holding her head together, her face swelling into a magenta water melon. Next, Angus kicked Henry O'Doherty in the groin shouting "For Bingo!"

As soon as the hypnotist O'Doherty was defeated some of the Conveniently-Out-Of-Copyright-Villains started waking up out of their hypnotic trances. Long John Silver and Professor James Eckhart were hugging each other as it turned out Silver was really Eckharts brother Elliot.

Gerald Macintosh, who had been acting like a warewolf, shook his head in confusion. Tim Eckleston said, "what's going on here?"

The battle raged for six-and-a-half-hours and was shown live on RTE and TV3. Some viewers compared it to the battle of Waterloo. The war zone had spread from the picnic area to all over the zoo, including the African Plains.

Here is the final summary of injuries:

11 bloody noses

65 broken bones

48 teeth knocked out

125 purple bruises

154 yellowy-green bruises

62 bite marks

257 scratches and grazes

391 uses of strong language

1023 uses of mild swear words

Half an hour after the battle ended the Gardaí turned up and arrested any of the villains who were still there: Humphrey Dunphy, Moriarty with his purple cravat badly torn, Dracula and the Wicked Witch of the West. The zoo keepers green clothes were torn and muddy. The cricketers' white clothes were destroyed.

Loretta's mum said she saw Merryweather escape in the direction of the Wellington Monument. Doctor Hervé

Chapeau de Guerre was never found, although his Admiral's hat was later retrieved from the Sumatran Tigers' enclosure and the zoo keepers later reported that the tigers were so full that they didn't need to feed them for a week.

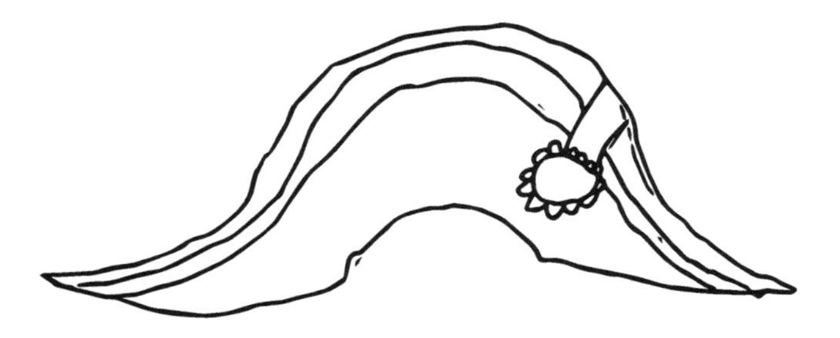

CHAPTER FOURTEEN

THE CHAPTER AFTER THE BIG BATTLE. MEDALS, EXPLANATIONS AND THE USUAL SET-UP FOR A SEQUEL

The Gardaí interviewed everybody and when they got to James Eckhart he showed them his ID card. He was a spy for S.P.E.C.T.R.U.M. (Special Executive for Counter Terrorism Run by Underage Minors). He had been spying on Doctor Chapeau de Guerre's fake institute for special robotics. His brother Eliot Eckhart had been captured and been hypnotised into believing he was Long John Silver.

Boris' father, Robert Quartermaine, arrived in a taxi as everyone was walking out through the main gate. He had missed the ferry home to Wales and stayed in the Travelodge for the few days.

"Hello father," said Boris.

"Hello Boris," said Mr Quartermaine. "The Police told me all about it. Do you want to go home now?"

"Am I in trouble?" said Boris.

"No Boris you are not in trouble, of course not. I heard you helped to save the day," said Mr Quartermaine. "Let's go back to Wales."

"You know the Wicked Witch of the West reminds me of someone we know," said Boris looking over where the lady with green skin was being arrested.

"She does, you know I'd know that face anywhere," said Mr Quartermaine. "Excuse me officer, can I see that lady for a moment please."

"Robert!" said the witch in a Russian accent.

"Ivana!" said Mr Quartermaine.

"Mother!" said Boris with great excitement offering her a thumbs-up.

After a few minutes the Garda had released Mrs Ivana Quartermaine and she was rubbing the makeup off her face and crying. She hugged her husband and Boris even let her hug him, just for ten seconds.

The O'Briens introduced themselves to the Quartermaines and invited them to stay in Cork for a holiday. Angus was whooping for joy at all his friends being alive. One of the Gardaí told him his father had been contacted. He was in Beijing on business but would fly straight to Dublin to collect Angus. Angus told the Garda his dad should fly to Cork instead because if Boris was going to stay with Loretta, he was going too.

The manager of the zoo came out and handed all of them life-long tickets to the zoo. Her sister arrived later and gave them tickets for a free holiday in Italy, all for saving the Zoo, the President of Ireland, and perhaps worldwide freedom.

Some trees were broken and others were still on fire. The zoo keepers did their best to get animals back in the right places. They put Gerald Macintosh in the wolf enclosure by accident, but they took him out later. The cricket team decided to give up cricket and formed a new type of martial arts based on their new battle skills. Tim , Stephen, Maurice and the other students all got back to their homes safely.

Two weeks later after a pleasant holiday in Cork Loretta, Angus, Boris, and their families (including Angus's brother Callum who had been rescued from the shed in Scotland) drove up to the Phoenix Park in Dublin again. As they drove past the Zoo they saw construction workers still fixing the trees, planting new trees, mending walls and fences.

They drove on past the Zoo to large white gates where they were greeted by James Eckhart wearing his S.P.E.C.T.R.U.M. ID badge which contained the toxic waste symbol. Boris thought it was a fidget spinner. Eckhart wore an expensive yellow suit, brown shoes, a green tie and pink shirt. Angus didn't recognise him at first as Eckhart was clean shaven.

"Come with me I need to introduce you to someone," he said.

Eckhart waved to the soldiers behind the gate who open it up and let them in. Eckhart said, "Welcome to Aras an Uachtarain."

"What does that mean?" asked Boris.

"This is where the President of Ireland lives," answered Loretta.

It was all very grandiose. Soon they were sitting around a large table with a full Irish Breakfast with luxury-range sausages; duck eggs; posh rashers; fine potato bread and award winning Black & White puddings approved by the food council of Ireland. The ketchup bottle was silver.

Eckhart had explained to the President that the three kids with special needs had saved him from being kidnapped by the League-Of-Conveniently-Out-of-Copyright-Villains.

The President asked Eckhart to bring the three kids into another room. He gave each one a medal for bravery.

After they left the President's house, before they all went back to Wales, Scotland and Cork, James Eckhart gave each of the three a permission slip and told them to get their

The President of Ireland

parents approval if they wanted to join S.P.E.C.T.R.U.M. (Special Executive for Counter Terrorism Run by Underage Minors).

Each of them thought about it and showed the slip to their parents. Eckhart spoke dramatically, “Chapeau de Guerre was only an underling. We need to find the real boss behind him. For 32 years I have been searching for the king pin of this whole operation. Will you help me track down and defeat General Volgen?”

“‘The Red Dragon says ‘yes!’” said Boris thumping the air and running around whooping. His Mum signed the form.

“Er ‘Captain Scotland, or Lord Edinburgh’ will come too,” said Angus flapping his hands excitedly. Mr McCreedie signed the form smiling at his son proudly.

“I don’t have a special hero name yet, but can I go as well mammy?” asked Loretta.

Her mother was crying again. Her father spoke (for the first time in this book, and when this is made into a film, the credits will be ready to roll), his voice was calm and mysterious.

“Go for it Illuminati Girl.”

THE END

The Tale of Harvey Duncan's Humiliation

Harvey Duncan from Dundee, Scotland won an expert puzzle-competition in the newspaper. The prize was the title of 'The most Intelligent Man in Scotland 1950'. On the 5th of July he attended the award ceremony in Edinburgh Castle. He went up onto the stage to receive the award from the King himself. Everyone he knew was there cheering him on. Then a man wearing a hat in the audience stood-up and said, "Harvey cheated, I can prove it. Here is the evidence!" Harvey denied it all until the evidence was examined. The crowd was appalled. The King said, "I was going to knight you, but now I must say, no king has ever been more ashamed of one of his subjects in the history of western civilization." Harvey trembled with his hands over his head, got down on his knees and crawled into a ball.

The End

Leonard, the Worst Hero of All Time

Leonard was walking along a footpath beside a big road in Queensland, Australia 3 June 1962. He saw an old lady walking across the road. There was a bus coming straight towards her. Leonard moved like a cheetah and pushed her out of the way of the on-coming bus. He braced for impact expecting the bus to bash into him and for the old lady to be saved from death. But the bus halted right in front of him as it was actually a bus stop. Then out of the corner of his eye he saw the old lady crumple over in front of a motorbike that was speeding along beside the bus. The bike driver shot over the handle bars and Leonard saw the coat and legs of the old lady whirling around as her head was caught in the front wheel. The motorbike driver screamed as he landed into the razor-sharp blades of a combine-harvester coming the other way.

The End

The Appalling Defenestration in Kerry

12-year-old Roger Conroy of Kerry, Ireland had a terrible temper. On 3rd May 1970 he lost a game of Snakes and Ladders to his brother Tom. Roger roared like a Lion and threw his dinner out the window. At that moment the parish priest Father Donal O'Shaughnessy, aged 53, came to the house collecting money for the poor. Roger's dinner plate spun quickly down through the air and sliced the priest completely in two, with slightly more of him on the left half than the right. The whole family were put into a mental facility.

The End

The Doughnut Debacle

In 1978 Luigi Gonzales set up a company making doughnuts in Quebec, Canada. Within ten years he had sold 1 billion doughnuts. The doughnuts were so popular that the Prime Minister of Canada said he loved them more than he loved his own wife. Five years later Luigi created the Wrestler Doughnut, a cartoon mascot on TV adverts. This was a big mistake because the voice for the Wrestler Doughnut was the most annoying voice in the world. Children and grown-ups hated it. Within a month, over thirty thousand people protested outside the factory every night. They held picket signs and pitch forks and torches. Every single person in Quebec signed a petition to force Luigi Gonzales to throw Wrestler Doughnut into the doughnut mixture and then fry him in boiling vegetable oil at his factory and make him into a real doughnut and then eat him, all live on TV.

August, Friday 13th 1993 was the night. Luigi sent out an actor dressed as Wrestler Doughnut to end the protest. But it went wrong. The lynch mob chased him into the factory where Luigi was ready with the TV cameras. Luigi was standing on a platform above the machine. The actor tried to run past him but the shoulders on his costume were very wide and Luigi was knocked off the platform. Gonzales arms grabbed the air as he fell, squealing like a pig and dropped into the mixture like a brick into a bathtub. The mixture splashed a bit and the crowd went silent. That day the doughnuts tasted a bit beefy. The actor and leaders of the mob were arrested.

The End

Hugh Smith Goes Too Far When he Forgets his P.E. Gear

Hugh Smith of Wellington, New Zealand, was aged 13. On the 5th December 1980, he was due to do PE (Physical Education) at Graham High School just after big break. As soon as the PE teacher entered the hall, Hugh realised he had forgotten his PE kit again. Mr Simpson the PE teacher said, "You know the rules Hugh. If you forget your PE gear you have to take the lesson in your underpants." The boys in the class laughed pointing at Hugh. Hugh throbbed with sudden rage and charged at the mustached, bespectacled figure of humiliation. At six metres away he pounced like a wolverine and ripped the teachers head off his shoulders with his clawing hands. The teachers body stood stupidly for a moment before gravity pulled it folding awkwardly to the floor. His neck squirting blood on the shocked boys who began to spew vomit. Hugh stood panting holding the severed head by the hair and roared like a dinosour. After a few minutes of roaring he came to his senses and realised he had got carried away and gone a bit too far. He decided to run away and live in the mountains as a wild man for the rest of his days.

The End

The Unfortunate Case of Monsieur Papier Perdu and the Misused Ticket

In 24 April 2003, French citizen Papier Perdu was catching a train from Berlin, Germany to Verona, Italy. Forty-five minutes before the train was due to leave nature called. He ran to the nearest public toilet, and went into a cubicle. Soon it was all over. He looked for toilet paper but there was none. He tried asking the person in the next cubicle for paper, but they didn't speak the same language. He searched his pockets and all he could find was the ticket. Oh dear, what could he do?

The End

Cannibalism in the USA

Nebraska, USA, 1998 saw terrible snow storms. Brandon and Jodie Nicholson were driving their pick-up truck with their two children Butch aged 9 and Joy aged 7. The storm was so terrible they crashed into another car. Unfortunately the other driver died, an old guy with a baseball cap and a goatee. Jodie stayed with the kids in the car who were crying with hunger. Brandon tried to call the emergency services but couldn't get a signal on his phone. Seven hours passed and no other cars had come down the road. The family were desperate. All they had was a camp stove in the trunk but nothing to cook. The radio said that rescue services in the area couldn't help for days. Brandon remembered a story about plane crash survivors who had to eat each other to stay alive. He looked at the other car with the frozen body of the old guy and had an idea. Half an hour later the family were feasting on a delicious stew made from the moose Brandon told his wife and kids he had caught. Just after they were finished they saw the flashing lights of the emergency services who had arrived, a little too late. Brandon never told his wife the truth.

The End

77324421R00063

Made in the USA
Columbia, SC
28 September 2017